Chancer the Dancer

Shelly Mack

Editor: Stephanie R. Graham
Cover Designer: Adinda Novalyawati
Illustrator: Adinda Novalyawati

Keep books alive!
Happy dancing :)
♡
Shelley

This book is dedicated to my brother, Bruce.

Thank you for being the best brother around, for your endless support, and for not only being a brother but a wonderful friend.

Love you always. xxx

In the leafy, green jungle
lives a monkey named Chancer.
He is brave and sweet
and a wonderful dancer.
He is quite famous
with his entertaining shows,
gathering up fans
wherever he goes.

His family of twenty
lives in a huge tree.
And everyone is welcome,
right down to the fleas.

But there is one animal
who never appears.
It's the fierce tiger
whom everyone fears.

Chancer puts on a show,
called *Chancer's Dance Moves*.
The animals cheer as he gets
into his groove.

Boys and girls at home, now is your chance.
Join in and show Chancer your special dance!

Put one hand high
and one hand low.
Move them up and down.
Here we go!

Let's do the monkey dance.
Let's do the monkey dance.
Let's do the monkey dance.
Ooh, ooh, ooh!

Let's do the monkey dance.
Let's do the monkey dance.
Let's do the monkey dance.
Me and you!

Out swinging one day,
Chancer hears a sound.
It is the tiniest of cries,
so he leaps to the ground.
He gracefully dances,
treading over so lightly.
There he finds two cubs
huddled in quite tightly.

Chancer leans in and says,
"Don't worry, it's all right.
I am very sorry
if I gave you a fright.
I have an idea!
Would you like to hear my song?"
The cubs nod as he says,
"You can even sing along!"

Boys and girls at home, now you know the song.
Get ready to sing and dance along!

Put one hand high
and one hand low.
Move them up and down.
Here we go!

Let's do the monkey dance.
Let's do the monkey dance.
Let's do the monkey dance.
Ooh, ooh, ooh!

Let's do the monkey dance.
Let's do the monkey dance.
Let's do the monkey dance.
Me and you!

No longer shy,
the cubs dance along.
Singing and giggling,
they join in with the song.

They all stop when Chancer
feels a rippling breeze.
Then, a thundering *ROAR*
comes from the trees.

A huge tiger appears,
and she stretches her jaws.
She walks over toward Chancer,
slowly flexing her claws.

Desperate to help Chancer,
the cubs run quickly to their mummy.
They tell her all about their day,
especially the song that was so funny.

Chancer says, "I'm sorry.
I only wanted to help.
I was worried when I heard
your little cubs yelp."

The tiger says, "Thank you!
What a kind thing to do.
Oh, how can I ever
make it up to you?"

Chancer says, "You're welcome,
but I need to go.
Maybe tomorrow
you can come see my show!"

The next day, the crowd gathers,
and Chancer looks out to see
that the tiger and her cubs
are sitting in the tree.

Chancer shouts out loud,
"I have a new song!
Please, everyone,
will you all sing along?"

Boys and girls at home, can you help by dancing along?
We will teach all my fans this brand-new song!

Bend your knees
and crouch down low.
Hold your hands like claws.
Here we go!

Let's do the tiger dance.
Let's do the tiger dance.
Let's do the tiger dance.
Roar, roar, roar!

Let's do the tiger dance.
Let's do the tiger dance.
Let's do the tiger dance.
More, more, more!

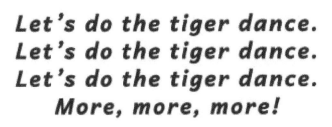

Everyone cheers
and dances along.
The applause is amazing
as Chancer finishes his songs.

As the tiger appears
the animals cower down low.
Then, they sigh in relief
when she says, "Hello."

Chancer beams in response.
Then, he gathers in the crowd
to introduce his new friends,
and they are welcomed aloud.
All the animals celebrate,
and friendships are made.
Now, everyone lives happily,
no longer afraid.

Acknowledgments

I would like to thank Frazer Nangle, Olivia Nangle, and Gracie Nangle. You three are my world.

To my editor, Stephanie R. Graham, I would be lost without you. You make me the best version of my writing self. Thank you.

To my illustrator, Adinda Novalyawati, you have been a wonderful find. Thank you for joining our team.

Thank you to my formatter, Manuel Garfio, as well as to my family: Colin Mackenzie, Cindy Mackenzie and Bruce Mackenzie.

Thank you to my friends Scott Grant and Louise Grant, who read all of my work and cheer me on. I would also like to give a special mention to Joanne Minto and Kirsty McQueen. You both have been a wonderful support system. Thank you for your friendships and for always having my back.

I would love to know what you think about *Chancer the Dancer*!
If you would like to read more Shelly Mack stories,
leave a little encouragement here:
Amazon
Goodreads
Facebook

Connect with Shelly Mack on social media and visit her website to sign up on the mailing list for book updates and competitions.

Website: www.shellymackbooks.co.uk
Instagram: @shellymackbooks
Twitter: @Shellymackbooks
Facebook: Shellymackbooks
Email: shellymackbooks@gmail.com

Books by Shelly Mack:

Go-Go the Gallimimus: A Dinosaur Tale

The Animal Series:

The Turtle and the Spider: A Very Sweet Adventure
Spikey the Hedgehog: The Big Accident

The Jungle Series:

Chancer the Dancer
Kellogz the Cornsnake (Coming Soon)

Germ Awareness Series:

Mr. Sniffles (Book 1)
Dot the Snot (Book 2 – Coming Soon)

Colouring and Activity Books:

The Turtle and the Spider: Colouring and Activity Book

Books available on Amazon, by Shelly Mack:

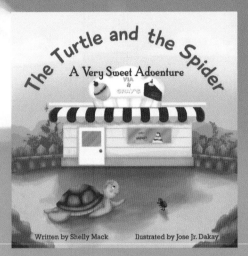

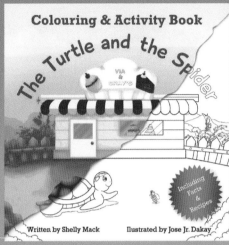

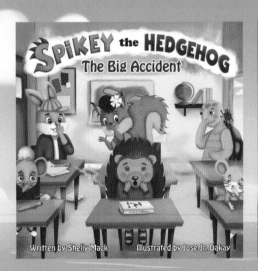

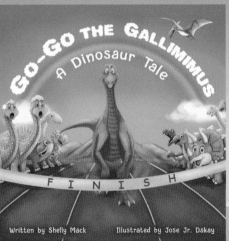

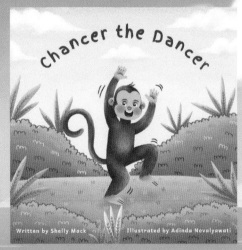

Printed in Great Britain
by Amazon